The Big Game

With special thanks to Mariam Vossough

To Bethany Kate Morgan

First published in paperback in Great Britain by
HarperCollins *Children's Books* in 2009
HarperCollins *Children's Books* is a division of HarperCollins *Publishers* Ltd,
77-85 Fulham Palace Road, Hammersmith, London W6 8JB.

Visit our website at: www.harpercollins.co.uk

1 3 5 7 9 10 8 6 4 2

Text copyright © Working Partners 2009
Illustrations copyright © Duncan Smith 2009

ISBN-13: 978-0-00-731039-5

Printed and bound in England by Clays Ltd, St Ives plc

The Big Game

JOE MILLER

Illustrated by Duncan Smith

HarperCollins *Children's Books*

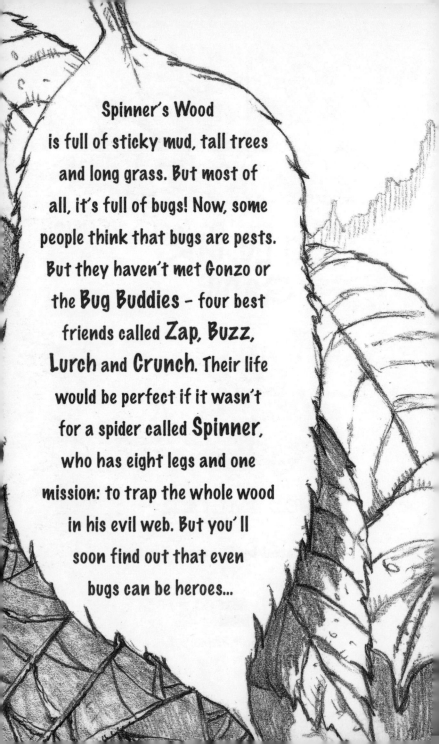

Spinner's Wood is full of sticky mud, tall trees and long grass. But most of all, it's full of bugs! Now, some people think that bugs are pests. But they haven't met Gonzo or the **Bug Buddies** – four best friends called **Zap**, **Buzz**, **Lurch** and **Crunch**. Their life would be perfect if it wasn't for a spider called **Spinner**, who has eight legs and one mission: to trap the whole wood in his evil web. But you'll soon find out that even bugs can be heroes...

Contents

CHAPTER 1

Zap zoomed through the air, his tiny wings buzzing. He was only a branch-length away from the apple now, but instead of slowing down he sped up.

"Watch out!" shouted Zap's friend, Lurch, who was watching

from a nearby rock.

But Zap wasn't going to stop
now. It was hard to find things to be
good at when you were no bigger
than a daisy petal. And this was the
one thing he was brilliant at – flying.
He was the fastest clover seed
weevil in Spinner's Wood.

"I can't look!" cried Lurch,
covering his eyes.

Just a bit closer… Zap told
himself. He got so near to the apple
that he could almost taste it. Then, at
the last moment, he darted around it.

"Oh no," he heard
Lurch cry.
"Zap got
splattered!"

Zap peeped
out from behind
the apple stalk.

"No, I didn't," he laughed.

"Oh, yeah, very funny," said
Lurch. "I thought you were
squashed. And who'd play centre
forward for the team then?"

"Charming," said Zap. He flew
down to the rock and landed beside

11

Lurch, who was tossing a dung ball in the air. Lurch was a shiny dung beetle

who used his legs to make big round balls out of poo, which he rolled around everywhere.

"Seriously though, you are an amazing flyer," said Lurch.

"Thanks," said Zap, backing away from the smell. He was used to his best friend carrying dung balls with him, but this one was particularly stinky. **"EW,"** said Zap, holding his nose. "Can't you put that somewhere else?"

"No! This is my best dung ball ever," said Lurch. "I'm going to call it Ploppy."

13

"Er… OK," said Zap. Lurch had never given a name to a dung ball before.

"Say hello to Ploppy," said Lurch. He turned to the dung ball. "And, Ploppy, this is my friend Zap."

"Lurch, you're talking to a ball of poo," said Zap.

Lurch grinned.

"Now, Zap," he said, "you really should stop being so horrible about yourself. You are **NOT** a ball of poo."

Zap sighed. He'd walked right into that one.

"I thought we could use Ploppy in the Beetle Ball final today," Lurch continued. "It's the perfect size for catching."

Beetle Ball! Zap's body tingled with excitement. He couldn't wait to play Centipede United in the big game later that day. But he didn't like the idea of playing with a dung ball.

"The ball's already been chosen," he said quickly. "We're going to use a pea seed."

Lurch's antennae sagged.

"This would be loads better," said

15

Lurch. "It's so easy to throw. Look."

He hurled the dung ball up in the
air, but it hit a branch above them.
The ball bounced from tree to tree,
disappearing into the forest.

"We've lost Ploppy!" wailed Lurch.

"Hmm," said Zap. "Shame. Now,
let's go to—"

"Zap!" said Lurch. "I need it back!
I'm a dung beetle."

Zap patted his friend on the back.
"OK, I'll go and look for it."

Zap spread his wings and whizzed
in and out of the trees, until finally
he caught up with the dung ball.
He darted in front and used his body
to stop the ball from going any
further. It came to a stop beneath a
bramble bush.

17

"Thank you for saving Ploppy,"
panted Lurch, as he caught up.

Zap coughed and spluttered,
wiping poo off himself with a leaf.

"My pleasure," he fibbed.

As he spoke, Zap felt a shiver
crawl through his tiny body. The air
had suddenly turned cold. He looked
around and realised that he didn't
recognise this part of
the wood. The trees
were taller here,
and Zap could hardly
see the sky at all.

18

He'd been so busy concentrating on the dung ball, he hadn't noticed where he was going.

"Where are we?" asked Zap.

The smile faded from Lurch's face as he looked around.

"I kn-kn-know where we are," he said, his six legs quivering with fright. "We're in **Shadow Creek**... where Spinner lives."

Zap laughed, trying to ignore the nervous feeling in his tummy.

"Spinner doesn't live here," he said. "He's just a made up story

to stop us flying too far from
home."

Lurch shook his head.

"He does live here," he said. "And
he's the meanest, scariest, bug-eating
spider in the world. **Let's get out
of here."** Lurch rolled his dung
ball away as fast as he could.

Zap hovered in the air, ready to
follow his friend. Just then, a gang of
black cockroaches crawled across
the rocks in front of him.

Cockroaches gave Zap the
creeps.

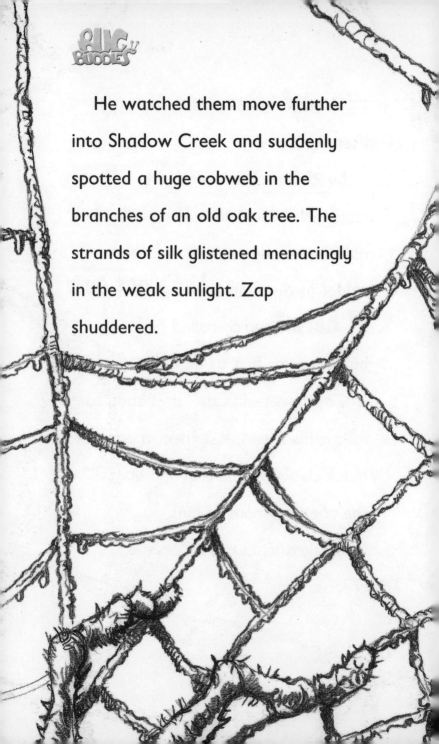

He watched them move further into Shadow Creek and suddenly spotted a huge cobweb in the branches of an old oak tree. The strands of silk glistened menacingly in the weak sunlight. Zap shuddered.

"Wait for me!" he shouted
after Lurch.

As Zap zoomed away, he
couldn't help feeling that his friend
might have been right.

Maybe Spinner *was* watching
them now!

CHAPTER 2

Back on the sunny side of Spinner's Wood, Zap flew close to the ground, whilst Lurch rolled his dung ball through the grass. Zap felt a pang of guilt as he spotted Gonzo the grasshopper waiting for them on his slab of rock.

"We'd better not tell Gonzo where we've been," Zap whispered to Lurch. "We don't want to get into trouble."

Zap had known Gonzo since he was a baby bug. Nobody understood more about Spinner's Wood than the grasshopper. He'd often warned Zap and his friends not to go near Shadow Creek.

As Zap landed, Buzz, a seven-spot ladybird, popped his head out from behind a stone.

"Hi guys, I was just having a snack,"

he mumbled, his mouth full of something.

"You're always having a snack!" said Lurch, laughing.

Gonzo gave Zap a long hard look. It was almost as if the grasshopper knew Zap had something to hide. Sometimes it felt as though wise, old Gonzo knew everything.

"Where have you two been?" asked Gonzo.

"Shadow C—" Lurch began. "Oops, I mean… nowhere…"

"Shadow Creek? Are you crazy?"

26

said Buzz, spitting out his food.

"Isn't that where Spinner's supposed to live?

He loves eating bugs like us!"

"We were chasing after Lurch's dung ball," Zap explained in a quiet voice. "We lost track of where we were."

Gonzo gave a sniff of disapproval.

"Rather than gallivanting in Shadow Creek, you should really do some training," he said. "It's your last chance before the match."

Zap felt a rush of excitement. This was the most important game he'd ever play! The Bug Buddies huddled together for a team talk, including Lurch and his ball of dung. Buzz backed away.

"But I thought we could use this in the game," Lurch said.

"**Ew!**" said Buzz. "I'm not playing Beetle Ball with **that!**"

28

"It's an interesting idea, Lurch,"
said Gonzo. "But perhaps you should
put it to one side while we practise."
Lurch hid the dung ball in some

29

long grass. Zap and the others
shared a relieved look.

"OK, team," said Gonzo,
clapping his front legs together,
"the bad news is that Wally the
wasp beetle is injured so we're one
player short."

Zap felt his little wings droop.

"We'll never beat Centipede
United now!" he said.

"Yeah," agreed Lurch. "They're
miles better than us. They've got all
those legs to run with."

"You'll just have to work extra

hard," said Gonzo. "Now, enough talking, let's get to it."

Zap felt nervous as they flew down to the training ground. Centipede United hadn't lost a game this year. Now the Bug Buddies had to face them in the final with one player down.

They would have to train like they'd never trained before!

CHAPTER 3

"Wow, this ball is slippery," said Zap, as he tried to pick up the shiny pea seed.

"The trick is to rub dry mud on to your hands," said Gonzo.

Zap scuttled over to a patch of mud and rubbed his tiny hands in the dust. Then he tried to pick up the ball again. This time he managed to keep a firm hold.

"We'll practise passing first," said the grasshopper. "Remember, the pea seed is light, so don't throw it too hard because you'll lose control of it. And remember **no flying** – that's cheating."

The bugs began to pass the ball around. The pea seed was the perfect size for Zap. It was so light he could run really fast with it. And it was easy for him to catch. *Perhaps we have a chance of winning after all*, he thought.

33

"OK," said Gonzo, "time to practise our special move. **The Zap Attack.**"

Zap groaned. They'd never managed to pull off this move and it was all his fault.

34

The Bug Buddies got into position.

Lurch hurled the ball down the field.

Buzz caught it and lined up to score.

But instead of going for goal he

quickly turned and threw it to Zap.

Zap was standing with his back to

the goal, facing Buzz. As the ball
came towards him, he spun upside
down and kicked the ball over his
head with his feet. But, as always…

…he completely
mis-hit it.

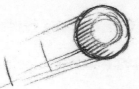

Instead of
going into the goal,
the pea seed sailed high up
in the air and disappeared into
the trees.

"Oh, stinky pond weed!" said
Zap, annoyed with himself for
missing again.

"Take a break while we try to
find the ball," called Gonzo, hopping
off into the wood.

Zap, Buzz and Lurch flew over
to Rotten Row, a line of dead trees

37

near the edge of the wood.

"There it is!" Lurch cried.

He started towards the seed,
which was lodged among the petals of
a primrose. But a gust of wind blew
him off course. He crashed into a
crumbling tree stump, where a large
beetle was hiding. Lurch fell on to the
ground and scrambled out of the way
as – **thunk!** – the beetle landed on
its back.

"Hey, what did you do that for?"
wailed the beetle, waving its legs.

Zap's eyes nearly popped out of

his head. It was the
scariest-looking
beetle ever, with
huge jaws like
antlers.

"Aren't you going to help me up?"
the beetle called.

Zap looked at his friends, unsure
what to do. That was one scary
beetle, but they couldn't leave it
stranded on its back. With trembling
wings, Zap flew over.

"Watch out!" cried Lurch. "It might
gobble you with those big jaws!"

"Please don't hurt me," pleaded
Zap.

"Don't be silly," said the big,
scary-looking beetle. "I don't want
to hurt you! I just want some help."

Zap hesitated. If the beetle really
was harmless, then he should turn it
over. But what if it was a trap?

Gonzo had always taught the
Bug Buddies to think the best of
other bugs, so Zap steeled his nerves
and landed next to the monster
beetle. Slowly, he reached out a
leg...

40

The beetle grabbed hold of Zap's leg and rolled itself over. Then it reared on to its hind legs and moved towards him.

"Thank you!" said the beetle. "And now you can be my **dinner!**"

Zap leaped backwards. **Oh no!**

"FLY, ZAP, FLY!"

screeched Buzz.

Hurrying to get away, Zap, Buzz and Lurch tripped over each other and fell into a heap. They cowered under their wings and waited for the beetle to strike.

It's all over, thought Zap. *I'll never play against Centipede United now.*

CHAPTER 4

Nothing happened.

Then Zap heard the big beetle laughing.
"Sorry about that. I love a good joke!"

Zap opened an eye. "You're not going to eat me?"

"Oh, no. I'm a stag beetle. I only eat tree sap."

As Zap got up, the stag beetle crawled straight past him and his friends. It used one of its large antlers to reach up and knock the pea seed from inside the primrose.

"Is this what you wanted?" he asked, throwing the seed so it landed neatly in front of Lurch.

"Thanks," said Lurch.

"You're welcome," said the

beetle. "My name's Crunch, by

the way."

Zap watched as Crunch's antlers

waved slowly through the air. *That*

was a perfect pass to Lurch, he

thought. An idea started to form in

Zap's head. If the stag beetle didn't

want to eat them, perhaps he'd like

to play with them? They were a bug

down, after all...

"Do you know anything about

Beetle Ball?" asked Zap.

45

"Are you kidding?" said Crunch.
"I love Beetle Ball!"

Zap waved his wings with
excitement. "Welcome to the team!"
he said.

Gonzo had been surprised to meet
the new member of the Bug Buddies.
But he soon admitted that Crunch
was a skilful player, even if his
running was a bit slow!

"Glad to have you on board!" he'd
said.

Now, beetles of every colour

had gathered for the Beetle Ball final. They lined the tall trees, waving their wings and hissing support for their teams.

There was a hushed silence as the referee, a very grand-looking Red Admiral butterfly, fluttered on to the field.

"Good luck. You'll need it!" teased the centipedes from their side of the field.

"We'll see," Zap whispered under his breath. He was determined to do everything he could to win this match.

The butterfly referee flapped his wings three times. This was the signal for the game to begin!

Straight away, Zap took the ball and zipped down the field. But Centipede United easily snatched the ball away from him and went scuttling towards the goal. The Bug Buddies tackled and dived but, no matter what they tried, they couldn't get possession of the ball. It was easy to see why Centipede United hadn't lost a match this year – they were brilliant!

Crunch nervously guarded the goal as a centipede took a shot at him. He threw his mighty antlers up to save it. But the ball whizzed straight between his claws and into the goal. The supporters cheered as Centipede United went one–nil up.

"This is impossible," said Buzz. "You never know which pair of their zillion arms and legs they're going to tackle with."

"Come on," said Zap, rallying his team, "we can't give up now."

The game restarted. Lurch grabbed

49

the pea seed and lobbed it towards the centipedes' half, completely forgetting Gonzo's advice not to throw it too hard.

"No!" shouted Zap as the ball flew over the treetops and into the distance.

Gonzo shook his head. Zap was upset – things were not going to plan. They were one–nil down already and now they'd lost the ball…

CHAPTER 5

Lurch pushed his dung ball forwards.

"Let's use Ploppy!" he said.

"Absolutely no way," said Buzz.
"I'm not touching that."

Zap looked at the dung ball
thoughtfully. It did stink and it was

sticky, but it was the right size and they could get a good grip on it…

Gonzo hopped over the ball. "Lurch is right," he said. "The dung ball is a good choice. You'll just have to cover your nose, Buzz."

Buzz sighed.

Gonzo called for the referee. The butterfly hovered over the Bug Buddies as Gonzo pointed to the dung ball.

"We obviously need a new ball and we'd like to suggest this one," he said.

The referee frowned. "That's a dung ball."

"Yeah!" said a centipede, who had wandered over to see what all the fuss was. "We're not playing with that."

Gonzo smiled. "I believe the rules state that any ball of approximately equal size and weight may be used for Beetle Ball."

"Oh, come on!" said the centipede.

"This stinks!"

"Yes," said the referee. "It certainly does. But it's not against the rules."

The butterfly flapped his wings three times.

"Play on!" he declared.

"Now, wait just a minute—" the centipede cried.

But it was too late. Buzz looked over at Zap and nodded. Zap raced towards the opposing team, clutching the ball of poo and holding his breath. The crowd cried out in delight. **Game on!**

Both teams were so desperate to score that they soon forgot all about the stink!

The ball flew from end to end as the players fired shots at the other team's goal. Again and again the ball was saved, to gasps from the crowd. Finally, Zap managed to break through the centipede defence and score a goal for the Bug Buddies!

It was one—one when the referee called half-time. Zap and his friends made for a small clearing in the woods to hold a team meeting.

"We can practise our Zap Attack in secret," Zap told them. Suddenly three cockroaches appeared in the clearing. Zap shared a nervous glance with his team mates. The last time he'd seen a cockroach had been in Shadow Creek.

"Great move," said one of them, shoving Zap.

"Yeah, you're the best," said another, nudging Buzz with his hard head.

Zap wished they'd told Gonzo where they were going. He looked around for help, but there were no other bugs to be seen. Zap saw his friends trembling and backing away from the strangers.

"Don't worry," he told the Bug Buddies in his bravest voice. But he was worried...

Looking for a way out, Zap spotted something that made him shiver. Hidden in the shadows behind a large tree, was a giant glistening web...

A spider's web...

Zap darted into the air. He realised that the nasty cockroaches were trying to push the bugs over towards the web.

Zap yelled to his friends.

"Get away! It's a trap!"

Crunch bravely raised his giant antlers to scare the cockroaches away. But the biggest cockroach gave Lurch one last push. Zap gasped as his friend stumbled backwards… straight into the web.

"Help!" Lurch cried, struggling in the sticky silk.

Eight long, hairy black legs began creeping out of the shadows towards the beetle.

Zap felt his wings shake in terror. His best friend was trapped!

CHAPTER 6

The biggest spider Zap had ever seen was crawling across the web towards Lurch. His body was the size of a pine cone. Sharp fangs hung from his gaping wide black mouth.

The giant spider turned towards Zap and glared at him.

"Ah," it spat. "A weevil. How sweet. Would you like to rescue your friend?"

Zap had never been so scared in his life, but he forced himself to answer.

"I **will** rescue him," he said.

The spider laughed, making the web shake. Lurch squealed in terror.

"I admire your courage. But I'm afraid you're too small and weak to help this dung beetle."

Clicking its fangs, the spider crept along the web towards Lurch, who quivered with fear. "My name is

Spinner," it hissed. "Nice to... **eat you!**"

Zap gasped. Spinner was real, and he was going to eat Lurch!

Lurch trembled. "Someone h-h-help me..." he begged.

"No one can help you now," gloated Spinner.

The cockroaches laughed as they watched from the grass. Buzz and Crunch flew up quickly to join Zap.

"What are we going to do?" said Buzz.

63

"What can we do?" replied Crunch, his antlers quivering. "Look at the size of him!"

But Zap didn't care how big Spinner was. He had to help his friend.

"There's one thing we can do that Spinner can't," said Zap. "Fly! On the count of three, we'll all fly at the web and rip it apart so Lurch can escape. I'd do it on my own, but I'm too small and light. **Together** we're strong."

"That's brilliant!" said Buzz.

Crunch backed away, shaking his head.

"I don't know," said Crunch. "I'm scared."

"So am I," said Zap. "But we can do this. We're a team, remember?"

Zap spotted Spinner edging closer to Lurch. His fangs glittered in the sunlight.

"Please, Crunch," begged Zap. "Remember when we first met you, and you said that bugs are always frightened by your big, sharp jaws?

We helped you even though we were scared. Now it's time for you to put those jaws to use – and help one of us!"

Crunch tapped his antlers together thoughtfully. "Yes…" he said. "I could bite through that web…"

Zap flew higher into the air. "Well, come on, then!"

Buzz and Crunch took off and the three of them flew towards Lurch, flapping their wings faster than ever before.

"Bug Power!" cried Buzz, as

they smashed through the web.

Crunch tore a massive hole, Buzz

managed a smaller tear

and Zap did his

best to rip the

web apart with

his tiny legs.

Each hole on

its own

wouldn't have been

enough to damage the web.

But the Bug Buddies had aimed

perfectly – the three holes

67

surrounded Lurch and the part of
the web where he was trapped
came loose...

"**No!**" cried Spinner as the silk
of the web frayed, then tore.

Suddenly Lurch was free and
he fell on to the ground. Spinner
snarled with fury and started to
lower himself down towards
the bug.

"**Lurch!
Start flying!**"

shouted Zap.

Dazed, Lurch managed

to fly up into the air just as Spinner swung towards him.

"There was no need to fly away. I was only coming to say hello," hissed Spinner.

"We know exactly what you were doing," said a grave voice.

GONZO!

Zap had never been more pleased to see the wise grasshopper.

"It's time you went back to Shadow Creek," said Gonzo as he hopped towards the giant spider. "You've been warned before."

Spinner hissed, but then to Zap's surprise he turned and crawled off

into the wood, his cockroaches following close behind.

"Will he be back?" whispered Zap.

"We'll have to be careful," said
Gonzo mysteriously.

A shiver passed through Zap as
the spider disappeared into the
shadows.

Chapter 7

When the Bug Buddies got back to the pitch, the centipedes taunted them.

"Oooh! Decided to come back, did you! We thought you'd run away!" they jeered.

Buzz glared at them. "Actually, we

were almost eaten by a great big
spider," he said.

The centipedes fell about laughing.
"A great big spider! Likely story.
You were running away, weren't
you? Running away because you
knew you were going to lose…"

Gonzo sprang into the air and
landed by the Bug Buddies. "That's
enough chat. Team – it's time to
teach these centipedes a lesson!"

73

Before long, there were only a few moments left to play, and the score was still drawn. Lurch passed the dung ball to Zap. But before Zap could catch it, the centipede captain barged in front and threw it down the field. The dung ball flew over Zap's head and headed towards the Bug Buddies' goal. The centipedes were about to score!

Zap zoomed along the pitch, zipping past the long brown centipedes. The ball started to curl downwards – heading for the back of the goal…

Zap dived to grab Ploppy. The ground hurtled towards him as he fell faster and faster.

"You're going to crash," shouted Lurch.

Zap wasn't going to give up now. He was determined to show he was as brave as a bug ten times his size. He stretched out and snatched the ball.

The crowd gasped as he fell back on to the grass.

He'd saved it! Zap would never have thought he'd be so happy to be crushed by a ball of poo!

He groaned and slowly stood up, holding the dung ball above his head. The crowd erupted into wild cheers.

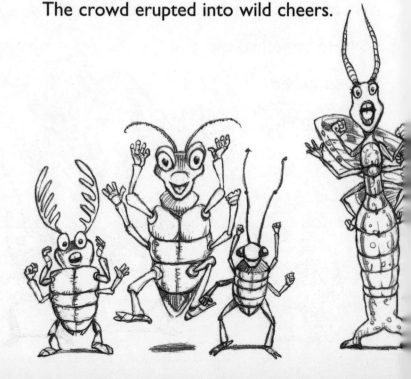

"Go, Zap! Go!" they cried.

Spurred on by Zap's bravery, the Bug Buddies got ready for one last attack on goal.

"There's only one thing for it," cried Lurch. "The Zap Attack!"

Zap's heart skipped a beat. Could he really do it?

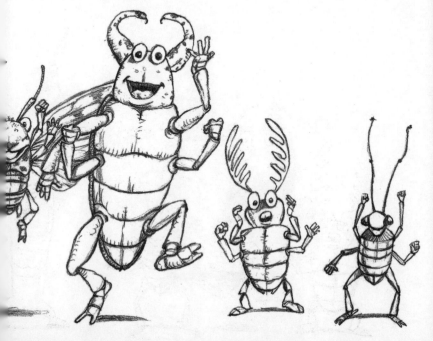

The Bug Buddies had already begun
their special move. Zap quickly took
up position with his back towards
the goal. His little heart pounded as
Buzz passed the ball to him. Zap
flipped upside down and kicked at it
over his head. *Please*, thought Zap,
just this once…

Everything seemed to go in
slow motion as he watched the
dung ball fly into the goal.

He'd done it.

The Bug Buddies had won!

CHAPTER 8

Zap was bursting with pride as the butterfly referee handed him the Acorn Cup. The Bug Buddies were now officially the **BEETLE BALL CHAMPIONS!** They celebrated their victory by taking it in turns to carry Zap on their backs around the field.

"Three cheers for the Bug Buddies!" called out a caterpillar.

"Hurrah! Hurrah! Hurrah!" shouted the bugs who had watched the game. After more celebrations, they headed to Gonzo's Rock. The old grasshopper was waiting there for them.

"Well done," he said, smiling.

"We are the champions," cried Buzz, running off to find a celebration snack.

Crunch and Lurch followed him, flapping their wings with joy. Zap stayed behind, clinging to the trophy.

"I can't believe this is ours," he said, staring at it in amazement.

"You deserve it," replied Gonzo. "You learned an important lesson today."

"That we can win a game with a ball of poo?" said Zap, jokingly.

Gonzo rolled his eyes.

"Yes… and that just because you're small, it doesn't mean you can't be brave. You stood up to Spinner and you won that cup. I'm proud of you."

Zap ducked his head to hide his blushes. When he looked back up he saw the grasshopper was gazing into the wood.

"One day your bravery will be tested again," Gonzo said, mysteriously.

Before Zap could ask what he
meant, Crunch crawled over and
lifted him up with his mighty antlers.

"We can't do our victory laps
without you," he declared.

Sitting on the stag beetle's back, Zap was caught up in his team's happiness. But as they raced around the field, he couldn't help casting an anxious glance over at Shadow Creek. Spinner was there, waiting for him. He could feel it…

With his friends cheering, Zap pushed that thought from his mind. Today had been the best day he'd ever had. He'd made a new friend in Crunch and his team had won the big game.

What more could a bug ask for?

STAG BEETLE

NAME: Crunch

FAMILY: Lucanidae

SIZE: 5 cm

HOME: tree stumps and logs in Spinner's Wood

LIKES: rotten wood, his friends, pretending to be scary

DISLIKES: flying, wrestling, arguments

CRUNCH

Stag beetles have a really long childhood and remain in the larvae stage for 3-5 years, snacking on rotting wood.

While the stag beetle is pretty scary looking, they mostly use their antlers to wrestle each other for female attention. Female stag beetles, however, will use their antlers to bite... so watch out!

LARVAE - The first stage of insect life

BUG BUDDIES

Enemy Attack!

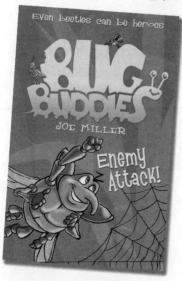

Spinner's Wood is under attack! The Bug Buddies think a certain spider is up to his old tricks. But is a new enemy on the prowl?

OUT NOW!

Turn over for a sneak preview of book two...

CHAPTER 1

Zap flew through the air, high
above the treetops.

Two of his friends, Buzz and
Crunch, sat on Gonzo's Rock,
cheering as Zap squeezed his tiny
weevil body through a small gap
between two branches.

It's now or never, thought Zap. He

turned upside down, before flipping

the right way up again. Then, beating

his wings with all his might, he did

another barrel roll.

Buzz the ladybird flapped his wings. "Wow," he said. "I've never seen any weevil do **tWO** flips!"

"You're little but **SO** brave," said Crunch, a big but not-so-brave stag beetle.

To be continued…

BUG BUDDIES

Ant Invasion!

Even beetles can be heroes

BUG BUDDIES

JOE MILLER

Ant Invasion!

It's party time and the yellow ants are happy to share their yummy food with the Bug Buddies. But is there something funny in the honey? What could the ants be up to...

OUT NOW!

BUG BUDDIES

Tunnel Trouble

JOE MILLER

Buy more great Bug Buddies books direct from
HarperCollins *Publishers*: at 10% off recommended
retail price. FREE postage and packing in the UK.

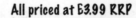